What Do Scientists Do?

HOUGHTON MIFFLIN HARCOURT

PHOTOGRAPHY CREDITS: COVER (bg) ©Jim Richardson/National Geographic/Getty Images; 3 (b) ©Ryan McVay/PhotoDisc/Getty Images; 4 (b) ©Kirill Kudryavtsev/AFP/Getty Images; 5 (t) ©Eliot J. Schechter/Getty Images; 6 (b) ©Peter Barritt/Alamy Images; 7 (b) ©Oleg Znamenskiy/Fotolia; 8 (b) ©North Wind Picture Archives/Alamy Images; 9 (t) ©Jim Richardson/National Geographic/Getty Images; 10 (t) ©Jochen Tack/Alamy Images; 11 (b) ©Fuse/Getty Images; 17 (b) ©Stockbyte/Getty Images; 19 (t) ©Science Source/Photo Researchers, Inc.

If you have received these materials as examination copies free of charge, Houghton Mifflin Harcourt Publishing Company retains title to the materials and they may not be resold. Resale of examination copies is strictly prohibited.

Possession of this publication in print format does not entitle users to convert this publication, or any portion of it, into electronic format.

Copyright © by Houghton Mifflin Harcourt Publishing Company

All rights reserved. No part of this work may be reproduced or transmitted in any form or by any means, electronic or mechanical, including photocopying or recording, or by any information storage and retrieval system, without the prior written permission of the copyright owner unless such copying is expressly permitted by federal copyright law. Requests for permission to make copies of any part of the work should be addressed to Houghton Mifflin Harcourt Publishing Company, Attn: Contracts, Copyrights, and Licensing, 9400 Southpark Center Loop, Orlando, Florida 32819-8647

Printed in U.S.A.

ISBN: 978-0-544-07334-0

3 4 5 6 7 8 9 10 1083 21 20 19 18 17 16 15 14

4500470073   A B C D E F G

Be an Active Reader!

Look for each word in yellow along with its meaning.

science	experiment	accurate
investigation	variable	spring scale
opinion	control	
evidence	balance	

Underlined sentences answer these questions.

What is a scientist?
Where do scientists work?
How do scientists investigate?
What happens when scientists observe?
How can models help scientists learn?
How do scientists plan an experiment?
How do scientists carry out an experiment?
Why do scientists display and share results?
What kinds of tools do scientists use?
What are some measuring tools?

What is a scientist?

What do you think of when you hear the word *scientist*? You might picture someone working in a lab. Some people think of a scientist as someone who studies animals or digs up fossils. All of these ideas are correct. Scientists do many things. Some even study space.

Science is the study of the natural world through observation and exploration. A scientist is a person who studies the natural world. Scientists work in every type of environment. However, they all follow similar steps as they observe and explore the world.

Scientists work in different settings as they study the natural world.

Where do scientists work?

Scientists work just about anywhere in the world, indoors and outdoors. Many scientists work in the field, or outside in nature. Botanists are scientists who study plants. They observe plants growing in nature. That might mean studying plants in a national park or on a nature preserve. It might mean looking at plants in a forest or jungle, or in a swamp or desert.

However, some botanists work in laboratories, too. Botanists might observe and compare plants from different environments. They collect data about how the plants grow and change under different conditions.

Botanists collect data about plants.

This meteorologist learns how storms form. He can track the storms on his screen. He can predict the direction a storm will move.

Other scientists also work in both field and lab settings. For example, a meteorologist studies the weather. Some meteorologists chase storms and collect data about temperature or air pressure. They may study cloud conditions. Meteorologists also work in laboratory settings. They use computers and other tools to track weather. Then they study the data and predict how the weather will change.

Scientists use similar skills in the field and in the laboratory. First, they observe. Then, they collect data. Scientists ask many questions about what they observe. They try to answer questions with an investigation. An investigation is a set of steps carried out to carefully observe, study, or test something in order to learn more about it.

How do scientists investigate?

One way scientists investigate is by observing things more than once. A single observation does not give enough information. Scientists must observe their subjects many times to check their observations.

A scientist may want to study a giraffe in its natural setting. The observations may make the scientist think of a question, such as "How do giraffes communicate?" The scientist will try to answer her question by observing the giraffes. She might observe the same group of giraffes over a long period of time. She might also observe giraffes over a wide area. Her repeated observations will help her learn about giraffes. She may soon be able to answer her question.

Scientists often study animals in natural settings. That way, scientists can learn how the animals behave in their environment.

Scientists use what they observe to make inferences. Inferences are conclusions based on observations. A scientist may observe that giraffes live in large herds. She sees that lions try to attack single giraffes that are away from the herd. She uses what she knows and what she observes to make an inference: giraffes live in large herds to stay safe.

An ==opinion== is a belief or judgment that is not based on fact. For example, one scientist may think that giraffes are beautiful. This is an opinion, not a fact. A scientific investigation must be based on evidence. ==Evidence== is information that has been collected, such as measurements. An opinion is not evidence, and it should never be part of an investigation.

Giraffes often stay in family groups.

What happens when scientists observe?

Scientists have always observed the natural world. Some people used to think the Earth was flat. But scientists kept observing the natural world. The Greek thinker Aristotle argued that the Earth is a round sphere. He used observations to prove his point. He noticed that a ship on the horizon viewed from the shore disappears from view as it sails away. But by climbing a hill or mountain, a person could see the ship again in the distance. This observation helped Aristotle make an inference. His inference was that the world was curved, not flat. Over time, scientists gathered data that proved the Earth had to be round. <u>Scientific observations increase our knowledge of the natural world.</u>

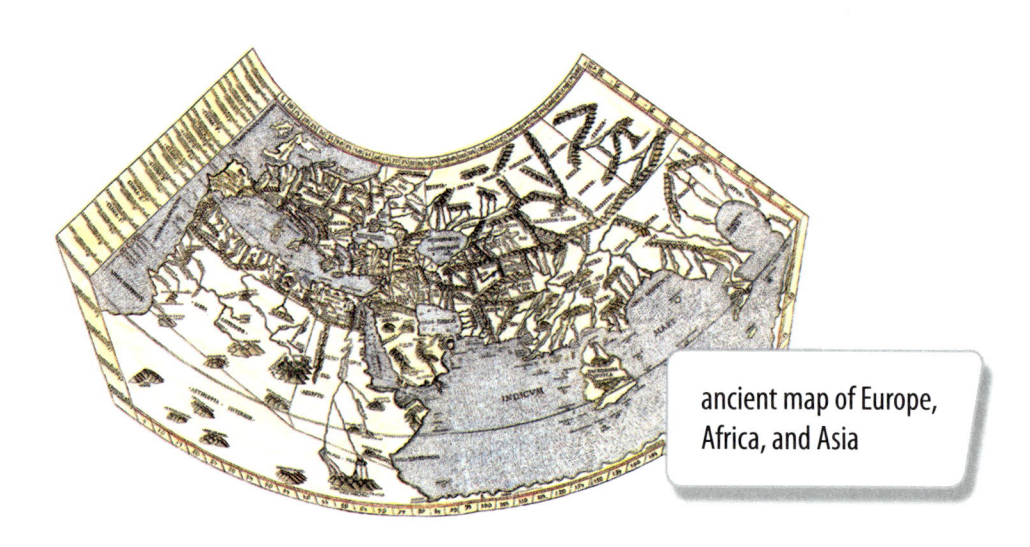

ancient map of Europe, Africa, and Asia

8

Today, tools such as powerful telescopes help scientists gather empirical evidence.

Empirical evidence is any data that can be observed or collected. Scientists gather empirical evidence and use it to show that they are correct about their ideas. They observe the evidence for themselves. Scientists cannot ignore new evidence, even if it requires them to think differently about things they once thought were true.

Our knowledge grows because of the observations of scientists. Today, scientists do not have to spend time investigating whether the Earth is round. They build on the discoveries and knowledge of scientists who lived long ago. They observe and learn new things about the world.

A model can show how objects relate to one another or how different parts make up a system.

How can models help scientists learn?

Have you ever built a model car or house? Scientists make and use models to investigate the world. A volcano might be too dangerous to explore. So, a scientist can make a model of a volcano. Stars and planets are too distant to explore. Scientists create models to show what planets look like.

Different types of models help scientists learn different kinds of things. A diagram shows how things are related, such as plants and animals in a food web. This kind of model shows the energy relationships between organisms.

A computer model can show changes over time. A model of a weather system can show where a storm system may be in a few hours.

A physical model helps scientists understand how something works. For example, a model of an insect can be made much larger than the actual insect. Scientists can use the model to understand the parts of the insect.

A model can be like the real thing in many ways. A model of a dinosaur might be the same size as a real dinosaur. But a model will be different from the real thing, too. A model of an atom will be much larger than an actual atom. A model of a heart will be made of plastic instead of real muscle. But such models are still useful.

Models help scientists understand how things work. Models can answer questions and help explain things that were not understood before.

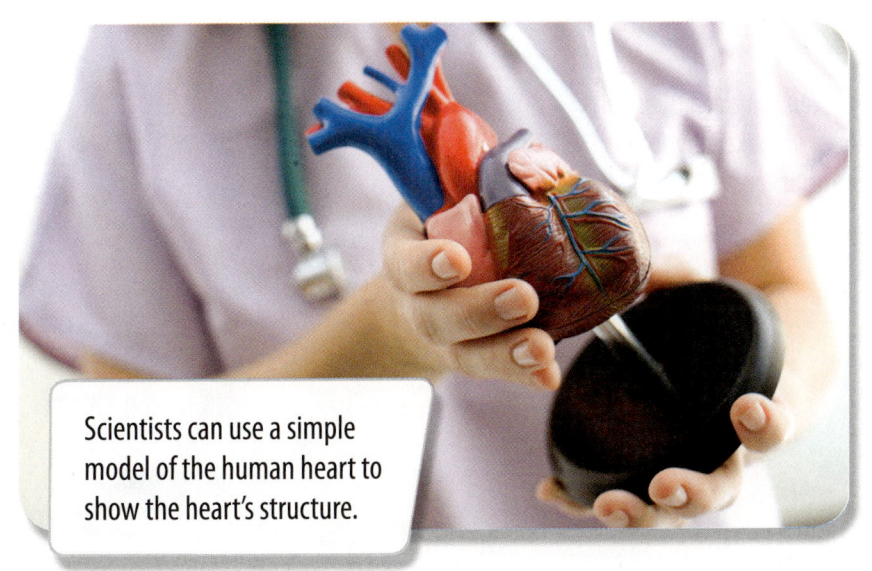

Scientists can use a simple model of the human heart to show the heart's structure.

11

How do scientists plan an experiment?

Scientists also learn about the world by doing experiments. An experiment is an investigation that sets out to test a statement called a hypothesis. Scientists follow a series of steps every time they perform an experiment.

The first step of an experiment is to ask a question. For example, you might ask, "How does the temperature of a magnet affect the magnet's strength?" The question must be something that can be answered by your investigation.

Next, form a hypothesis. A hypothesis is a statement that explains a set of facts. It is a way of saying what you think might be true. A hypothesis must be able to be tested. Your hypothesis might be, "A warm magnet will be stronger than a cold magnet."

You can ask a question and make a hypothesis that can be tested.

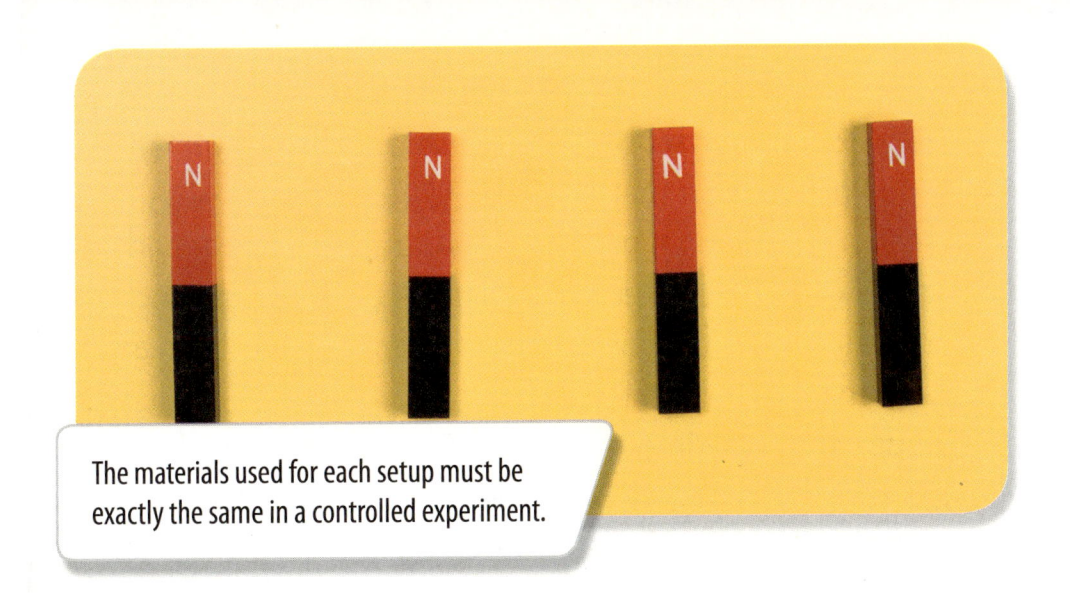

The materials used for each setup must be exactly the same in a controlled experiment.

Next, make a plan that will test your hypothesis. The variable in an experiment is the thing that will change. In your magnet experiment, the variable is the temperature of the magnets. Everything else will stay the same. Testing only one variable makes it clear what causes any changes that occur in the experiment.

When scientists design an experiment, they make one part of the experiment the control. In the control, no variables are changed. The use of a control makes it easier to tell why something happened in an experiment. In the magnet experiment, the magnet that is at room temperature is the control. You will compare the hotter or colder magnets to it.

13

How do scientists carry out an experiment?

Every experiment requires similar steps. Make a plan and follow it. Prepare your materials.

Use four identical magnets. Place one in the freezer and one in the refrigerator. Keep one at room temperature and place one in hot water. Think about safety. Get help from an adult when using hot water.

Set up your experiment carefully. Place the four magnets next to each other, facing the same direction. Take the temperature of each magnet, and record it. Then place a paper clip 15 centimeters (about 6 inches) away from each magnet. Move each paper clip closer to its magnet 3 centimeters at a time. Record which paper clip was attracted to a magnet at the greatest distance away.

Do the experiment exactly the same way each time. Record your measurements.

Record data accurately during your experiment. You will analyze the data later.

Look at your data and see how it answers your question. You found that the magnet at room temperature attracted a paper clip from the greatest distance. This means it was the strongest magnet. The paper clip was 8 centimeters (three inches) away when it moved toward the magnet. Your results show that temperature *does* affect the strength of a magnet. It is okay that your results did not support your hypothesis exactly.

The other magnets became weaker when their temperatures changed. Repeat the experiment to make sure you get similar results. When you repeat an experiment and get similar results, you know that the results you got are reliable.

Why do scientists display and share results?

The next part of an experiment is to communicate the results. Sharing results helps others learn from what you found out. They may decide to test your results with their own experiment. Sharing results with others might also help you draw new conclusions about your work.

Tables, charts, and graphs display results of an experiment. Displaying results helps you organize information in a visual way. Be exact about your measurements. Include all of the information you know.

A chart displays word data. Tables display data in numerical, or number, form. Line graphs show change over time. Circle graphs compare parts of a whole. Bar graphs compare things or groups of data.

	Control 21.1 °C (70°F)	Freezer −17.7 °C (0 °F)	Refrigerator 1.6°C (35 °F)	Heated 37.7 °C (100 °F)
Centimeters from magnet that paper clip was attracted	8	3	5	1

You must accurately record how far away each paper clip was from its magnet before it was attracted to the magnet.

How might a scientist think critically and draw a conclusion about the experiment with magnets? We have seen that magnets do not perform as well if they are not at room temperature. Your results can help you infer that magnets should not be stored in either a hot place or a cold place.

The experiment also tells us something about how magnets must be used in the real world. Magnets are often used in machines in factories. If these magnets get too hot, they will not perform well. Engineers must keep this in mind when they are designing factory machines that use magnets.

Powerful magnets must be designed so that they will work in factory settings, where machinery often heats up.

What kinds of tools do scientists use?

Scientists use many tools to collect data. Some tools are used for observing. Collecting nets and specimen jars are used to gather living things. Hand lenses help scientists see small things up close. A camera can record an image of something that cannot be collected, such as a tree. A video camera can record actions and events, such as a forest fire.

Metric rulers, tape measures, and calipers measure the length of objects. Clocks, stopwatches, and timers measure time. Thermometers measure temperature.

It is important to think of safety when using any kind of tool for science. Gloves can be used to handle objects. Goggles protect eyes. Scientists must think about safety both in the field and in the laboratory.

Tools and safety equipment help scientists make observations in the field and in the lab.

A scanning electron microscope makes an object look thousands of times larger than it really is.

Scientists in a laboratory use different tools than field scientists do. A light microscope helps laboratory scientists see things that are very small. A small part of a plant or an animal can be seen magnified many times with a light microscope.

A scanning electron microscope shows things that are extremely small, such as tiny structures inside the living cell of an organism.

A dropper helps move liquid from one container to another. A pipette can measure very small amounts of liquids.

Scientists choose the tool that will best help them to gather and observe data.

19

The reading on a pan balance is accurate when both sides of the balance are even.

What are some measuring tools?

Mass is the amount of matter in an object. The unit used to measure mass is called a gram. A balance is a tool that measures mass. There are different kinds of balances. A pan balance has two sides. To use a pan balance, place an object in one of the two pans. Then place small gram masses in the other pan. Continue until both sides are balanced. The beam should be completely level. The total of the gram masses tells the mass of the object in the other pan. A balance is a very accurate, or exact, way to measure matter. An electronic balance gives a digital reading of an object's mass.

Scientists can also measure force on an object. The unit used to measure force is called a newton (N). A spring scale is a tool that is used to measure force on an object. Attach the end of the scale to the object being measured. Then pull the spring scale slowly up into the air or along a surface. The spring extends to a point along the scale.

Scientists use many tools to explore the natural world. These tools can also help in investigations. As scientists observe, build models, and conduct controlled experiments, they gain new knowledge. They use logic to think critically about the world. This kind of thinking can lead to new investigations. It can lead to new discoveries about science.

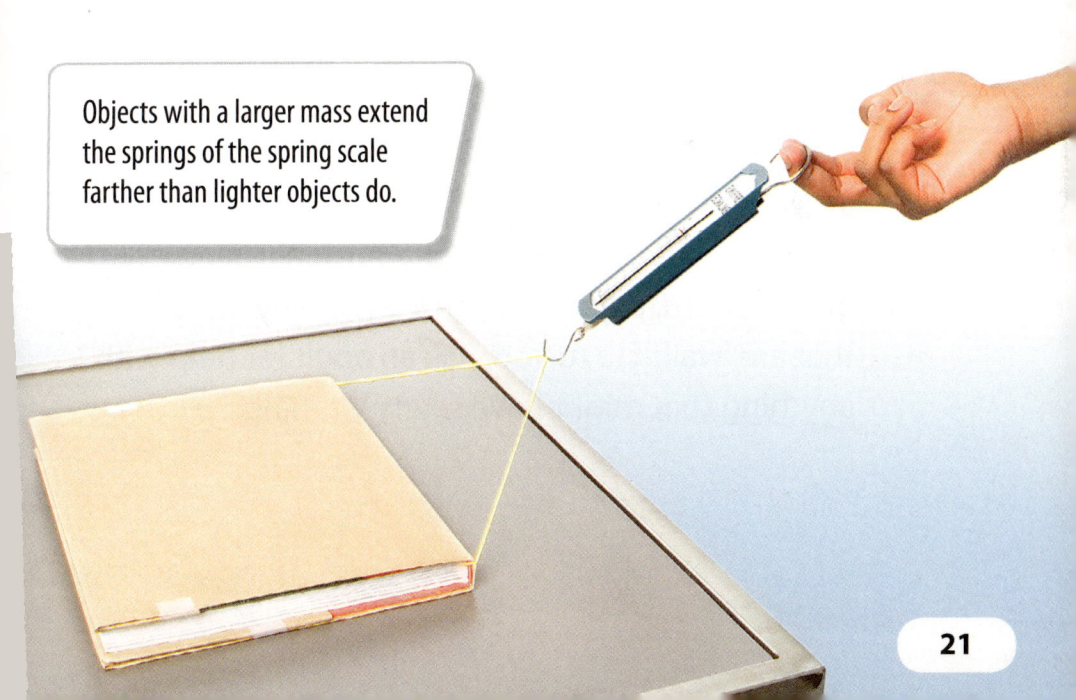

Objects with a larger mass extend the springs of the spring scale farther than lighter objects do.

Responding

Ask a Question and Investigate

With a partner, choose something in nature on which to conduct an experiment. You may want to observe a tree, insect, or rock. Get your teacher's approval to carry out your experiment. Take notes, draw pictures, or take photographs. After you have gathered your data, come up with a question about what you found. Form a hypothesis to answer your question. Then test your hypothesis. Present your results visually in a chart or poster. Explain why you think you got the results you did.

Make a Model

Work with a partner. Make a model of something you observe in your everyday life. Get your teacher's approval for your project. Your model can be a diagram, or it can be three-dimensional, made out of cardboard, papier-mâché, clay, or any materials that are available to you. Ask an adult for help with anything that might have safety warnings.

Glossary

accurate [AK•yuh•ruht] In measurements, very close to the actual size or value. *A ruler gives an accurate reading of the length of an object.*

balance [BAL•uhns] A tool used to measure the amount of matter in an object, which is the object's mass. *The balance shows that the ball is five grams.*

control [kuhn•TROHL] The experimental setup to which you will compare all other setups. *It is easier to understand the results of an experiment when there is a control.*

evidence [EV•uh•duhns] Information collected during a scientific investigation. *Measurements are often used as evidence in scientific investigations.*

experiment [ek•SPAIR•uh•muhnt] An investigation in which all of the conditions are controlled to test a hypothesis. *You can experiment to find out which magnet is strongest.*

investigation [in•ves•tuh•GAY•shuhn] A procedure carried out to carefully observe, study, or test something in order to learn more about it. *An investigation is a good way to learn about the natural world.*

opinion [uh·PIN·yuhn] A personal belief or judgment based on what a person thinks or feels but not necessarily based on evidence. *Sarah's opinion will not get in the way of her scientific findings.*

science [SY·uhns] The study of the natural world through observation and investigation. *When we use science, we find out about the world around us.*

spring scale [SPRING SKAYL] A tool used to measure force. *The book moved the spring scale farther than the cup did.*

variable [VAIR·ee·uh·buhl] Any condition that can be changed in an experiment. *It is important to change only one variable at a time in an experiment.*